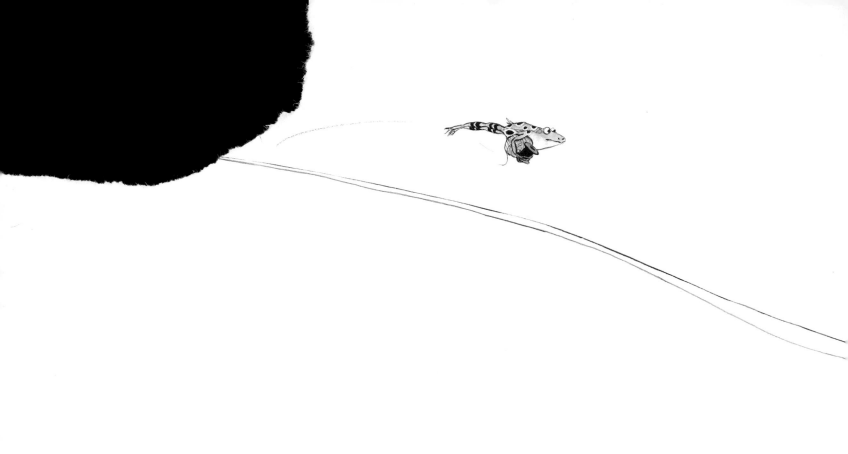

Library of Congress Cataloging-in-Publication Data   Gretz, Susanna.   Frog, duck, and rabbit / Susanna Gretz. — 1st American ed.
p.   cm.   Summary: Three animal friends make a costume for a parade.   ISBN 0-02-737327-4   [1. Animals—Fiction.
2. Cooperativeness—Fiction. 3. Friendship—Fiction.]   I. Title.   PZ7.G8636Fs   1992   [E]—dc20   91-16364

Frog, Duck, and Rabbit

Susanna Gretz

Four Winds Press   New York

Maxwell Macmillan International
New York   Oxford   Singapore   Sydney

Frog, Duck, and Rabbit are making a costume.

"It will need wheels," says Duck. "I'll get my skates."

"Stupid skates," says Rabbit.
"They're not," says Duck.

"Your feet look stupid, too," says Rabbit.
"They don't," says Duck.
"Flatfoot, Flatfoot!" says Frog. "And if you can have wheels, so can I."

Frog gets her scooter.
"Stupid scooter," says Duck.
"It isn't," says Frog.

"Your spots look stupid, too," says Duck.
"They don't," says Frog.
"Spottybotty, Spottybotty!" says Rabbit.
"And if you can have wheels, so can I."

Rabbit gets his skateboard.
"Stupid skateboard," says Frog.
But Rabbit isn't bothered.

"Your ears look stupid, too," says Frog.
Rabbit still isn't bothered.

"Flopears, Flopears!" says Duck.
Now Rabbit *is* bothered.
"Don't call me that," he says.

"Anyway," says Frog, "*you* started the teasing, Rabbit."
"No, I didn't," says Rabbit.
"Yes, you did, Flopears!"

"My name isn't Flopears!" yells Rabbit.
"Flopears, Flopears!" yell Duck and Frog.

"STOP!" wails Rabbit.

Suddenly, they remember the costume.
"It's nearly time for the parade," says Duck.

"And we haven't even *started* on the costume,"
moans Rabbit.
"Let's get busy," says Frog.

They work very hard.

Finally the costume is ready.

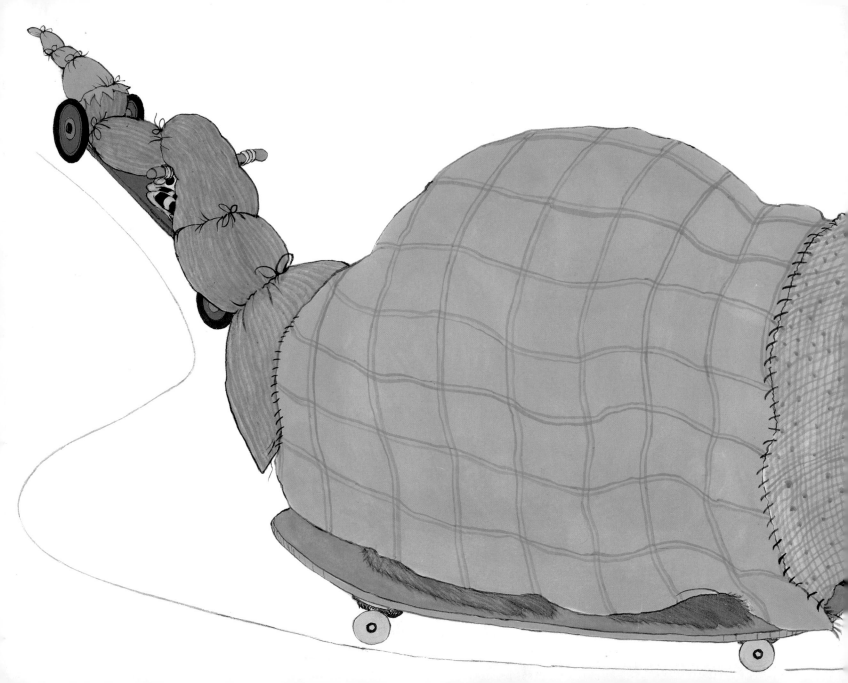

It's the best crocodile . . .

. . . in the whole parade.

Everyone admires the costume on wheels.
"Did you make it yourselves?" they ask.
"Yes," says Rabbit." It was made by Flatfoot,
Spottybotty . . ."

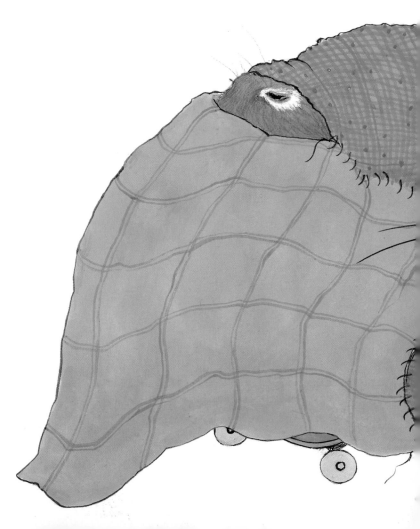

"What?" yell Duck and Frog.

"... and Flopears," says Rabbit.

And then Flatfoot, Spottybotty, and Flopears
go home for their tea.